The Musicians
of P

ADAPTED FROM
JACOB AND WILHELM GRIMM

Pictures by J. P. MILLER

SIMON AND SCHUSTER
NEW YORK

THE LITTLE GOLDEN BOOKS ARE PRODUCED
UNDER THE SUPERVISION OF
MARY REED, Ph.D.
FORMERLY OF TEACHERS COLLEGE,
COLUMBIA UNIVERSITY

This old German folk tale has been illustrated especially for Golden Books by J. P. Miller, whose newest books include THE BRAVE LITTLE TAILOR and PUSS IN BOOTS. These are part of a group of Little Golden Books designed to bring the best folk and fairy tales to children everywhere.

THERE ONCE was a donkey, who had faithfully carried his master's corn to the mill for many years. Now he was too old to do the work, so his master planned to get rid of him.

The donkey knew that, so one day he stole away from the farm.

"I like to sing," he thought to himself, "and many have said I have an extraordinary voice. I think I shall go to Bremen and become a town musician."

So he started off toward Bremen.

He had not gone far when he came upon a hound, lying by the road and panting heavily.

"What is the matter?" the donkey asked.

"I have run away from home," explained the hound. "Because I am old and can no longer hunt, my master wants to do away with me."

"Come with me," said the donkey. "I am going to Bremen to be a musician there. You can, too, for everyone knows what fine voices you hounds have."

The hound agreed, and joined the donkey.

Together they walked until they came to a cat, sitting by the roadside all by herself, with a face as gloomy as three rainy days.

"Here now, friend, what has gone wrong with you?" the donkey asked.

"Because I am old and can no longer catch mice, my mistress wants to do away with me," mourned the cat. "So I have run away. But I do not know where to go."

"Come with us to Bremen," the donkey said. "We

are going to be musicians there. You so often sing at night.
You can be a Bremen town musician too."

The cat thought this was a good idea, so she went
along with them.

Down the road the three runaways came to a farm,
and there on the fence sat an old cock, crowing with all
his might.

"Whatever is the matter?" the donkey asked.

"My mistress has told the cook to make stew of me for Sunday dinner, so I am crowing while I can," said the cock sadly.

"You had better come away with us," the donkey said. "We are going to Bremen to be town musicians. With your voice I am sure you would be a great success."

The cock agreed, so the donkey and the dog and the cat and the cock went along together.

When night fell, they found themselves deep in a forest. The donkey and hound lay down to sleep at the foot of a big tree, while the cat and the cock settled themselves in its branches.

As he was just about to close his eyes, the cock saw a light burning not far off.

"Hallo, friends," he called, "I see a window light."

"Let us find out what kind of a house is there," said

the donkey. "Perhaps we may find food and better shelter for the night."

So they made their way through the woods to the house, and they looked in the window.

What do you think they saw inside? They saw a band
of robbers around a table loaded down with good things
to eat. How warm and well-fed those robbers looked to
the hungry animals!

"We must think of a plan to drive them away," said
the donkey. "Then we shall have good food and warm
beds."

So the musicians put their heads together and at
length came up with a plan.

The donkey stood with his forefeet on the window sill. The hound leaped to his back. The cat climbed up to the hound's head, and the cock fluttered up to perch on the cat.

At a signal from the donkey, they all began to sing as loudly as they could. The donkey brayed, the hound barked, the cat meowed, and the cock crowed lustily. What a noise!

Then they burst through the window, frightening the
robbers so badly that they all ran away into the forest.

The four musicians sat themselves down at the table for a fine dinner. When they were finished, they put out the lights, and each found a sleeping place that seemed comfortable to him.

The cock flew
up onto the roof.

The cat curled up on the warm hearth.

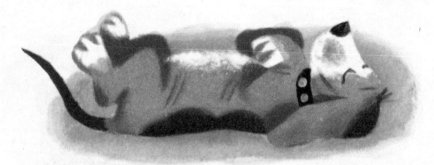

The hound stretched out behind the front door,
and the donkey lay down on some straw in the yard.

Now all was quiet and the four companions slept. But out in the forest the robber band decided they had been too easily frightened away. So when they saw the lights go out, back went the boldest of them all, to find out what had happened.

The robber crept into the house, and finding everything quiet, he knelt down to the hearth for coals to light a candle. But what he took to be live coals were the fiery eyes of the cat. Up she sprang and flew at the robber, spitting and scratching him.

The frightened robber ran for the door, but there he fell over the dog. The hound bit him in the leg and sent him stumbling out into the yard. There the donkey kicked him soundly with his hind feet.

As the robber ran into the forest, the cock awoke on his rooftop perch and crowed, "Cock-a-doodle-doo!"

Panting and trembling, the robber came back to his band.

"What happened? What happened?" they cried.

"There was a witch in the house," the robber said. "She spat on me and scratched me with her long nails. Then a man by the door stabbed me with a knife, and a monster in the yard clubbed me as I went by. And on the rooftop sat a judge, who cried, 'Bring the rogue here!' We dare not go back to that house!"

And so the robbers went away, leaving behind their food and their gold. But the house suited those four musicians so well that they never did go on to Bremen. Instead they lived happily on in the house in the woods, and gave musical concerts for themselves, which they all enjoyed mightily.